Will   Irma   Taranee   Cornelia   Hay Lin

GRAPHIC NOVEL #5
LEGENDS REVEALED

W.i.t.c.h.

Will   Irma   Taranee   Cornelia   Hay Lin

GRAPHIC NOVEL #5
LEGENDS REVEALED

HYPERION PAPERBACKS
FOR CHILDREN
New York

© 2006 Disney Enterprises, Inc.
W.I.T.C.H., Will Irma Taranee Cornelia Hay Lin is a trademark of Disney Enterprises, Inc.
Hyperion Paperbacks for Children is an imprint of Disney Children's Book Group, L.L.C.

Printed in the United States of America

First Edition
1 3 5 7 9 10 8 6 4 2

ISBN 0-7868-4876-6

Visit www.clubwitch.com

I HOPE YOU HAVE **YOU-KNOW-WHAT** IN THAT BACKPACK OF YOURS!

OF COURSE I DO, MRS. KNICKERBOCKER!

WOULD YOU ALL EXCUSE ME?

WINK

WELL, IT'S NOT PERFECT... THE COLORS... QUALITY...

LET ME BE THE JUDGE OF THAT!

IT'S REMARKABLE! YOU HAVE A GREAT TALENT, HAY LIN, AND I THINK YOU SHOULD SHARE IT WITH YOUR CLASSMATES.

WHAT DO YOU MEAN?

AS YOU KNOW, THE DRAMA CLASS WILL BE PUTTING ON A HOLIDAY PLAY. OUR SCHOOL HAS A MULTIETHNIC TRADITION, SO...

WHAT WOULD I HAVE TO DO?

...THIS YEAR'S PERFORMANCE WILL BE DEDICATED TO LEGENDS FROM AROUND THE WORLD.

WHAT IS IT THIS TIME?

IF HE LIFTS UP MY ROOTS, YOU'LL BE ABLE TO SEE MY SHOES!

THIS IS JUST A REHEARSAL, LENNY! FORGET ABOUT YOUR SHOES! THE AUDIENCE WON'T NOTICE THEM!

NO ONE WILL NOTICE ME ANYWAY! BECAUSE THIS PART IS TOO SMALL!

I DON'T WANT TO BE THE TREE!

THEN DON'T DO IT. THERE ARE LOTS OF PEOPLE OUT THERE WHO'D BE WILLING TO TAKE YOUR PLACE!

LIKE ME, YOU MEAN?

COME ON, HARRY! YOU'RE ALREADY PLAYING THE SHRUB.

WELL! LOOKS LIKE OUR HAY LIN IS REALLY SHOWING HER TRUE COLORS!

IT'S TOUGH TO MAKE EVERYONE IN A SCHOOL PLAY GET ALONG!

THE TRUTH IS, YOUR STORY'S JUST PLAIN SILLY!

HMMM . . . LISTEN TO THAT!

SOUNDS LIKE TROUBLE'S BREWING IN THE REHEARSAL HALL.

YOU LOOK WORRIED, IRMA! ARE YOU AFRAID YOU WON'T DO WELL IN THE TRYOUTS, OR ARE YOU JUST SCARED OF THE COSTUMES HAY LIN'S GOING TO DESIGN FOR YOU TO WEAR IN THE PLAY?

HUH?

OH, DON'T GET UPSET! I'M SURE IRMA WAS JUST EXAGGERATING WHEN SHE SAID YOU HAD HORRIBLE TASTE!

GRRRRR!

IRMA!

THAT'S NOT TRUE! I NEVER SAID ANYTHING LIKE THAT!

AND I THOUGHT YOU WERE MY FRIEND!

B—BUT... BUT...

12

TAKE IT BACK, CORNELIA, OR... OR...

DON'T BE RIDICULOUS! YOU'RE NOT GOING TO BELIEVE THOSE TWO TROUBLE-MAKERS, ARE YOU?

IT'S GETTING LATE. WE'D BETTER GET GOING...

YEAH, YOU'D BETTER.

HEY, TARANEE! YOUR BROTHER'S HERE.

HUH?

PETER! WHAT ARE YOU DOING HERE?

JUST BEING YOUR DELIVERY BOY. YOU FORGOT SOMETHING WHEN YOU LEFT THE HOUSE!

WILL'S RIGHT! I WANTED THE PLAY TO BE A SURPRISE...

BUT MAYBE THE TIME HAS COME FOR YOU GUYS TO KNOW THE WHOLE STORY OF THE FOUR DRAGONS.

SOUNDS GOOD. BUT WHY RIGHT NOW?

JUST LISTEN AND YOU'LL UNDERSTAND. I COULDN'T BELIEVE IT MYSELF WHEN MY MOM TOLD ME.

OKAY, HAY LIN, I'M CURIOUS... SO, BEGIN. WE WERE AT THE PART ABOUT THE PEOPLE BEING HUNGRY.

RIGHT! THE DRAGONS DECIDED TO HELP THEM, AND IT WAS THE RED DRAGON WHO FIGURED OUT HOW.

THE SEA! ALL THE WATER WE COULD WANT IS THERE! AND WITH THAT WATER, WE COULD HELP THOSE PEOPLE!

WE JUST HAVE TO SCOOP IT UP IN OUR MOUTHS AND SPRAY IT INTO THE SKY OVER THEIR FIELDS! IT WILL TURN INTO RAIN AND FALL ON TO THE CROPS!

HERE IS MY ORDER TO THE MOUNTAIN SPIRIT WHO *WILL* OBEY ME . . .

LOCK THESE DRAGONS UP IN FOUR SEPARATE MOUNTAINS! MAKE SURE THEY WILL NEVER BE ABLE TO LEAVE!

BUT WE ONLY DID WHAT WAS RIGHT!

THE EMPEROR HAD NO PITY FOR THE DRAGONS, AND HIS ORDER WAS CARRIED OUT.

19

YOUR ORDER HAS BEEN OBEYED, YOUR MAJESTY!

THIS IS WHAT HAPPENS TO THOSE WHO ROUSE MY ANGER!

NOW THEY WILL NEVER BE ABLE TO *DO GOOD*, EVER AGAIN!

HMMM . . .
A BIT LONG, BUT POETIC.
NO ARGUMENT THERE.

WHAT DO YOU THINK ABOUT
THAT? DRAGONS! NYMPHS!
THAT'S WHAT I THINK OF AS
REAL MAGIC!

WHAT DOES THAT MEAN?
THAT YOU THOUGHT OUR
MAGIC WASN'T REAL?

YOU KNOW SOMETHING,
HAY LIN? YOUR
COSTUMES AREN'T SO
BAD AFTER ALL!

THANKS, IRMA . . .

BONK

TO HECK WITH THE
GRUMPERS! MY MOM ALWAYS
SAYS RUMORS NEED A SHARP
TONGUE . . .

23

BUT THEY ALSO NEED
A WILLING EAR! MY MOM
SAYS THAT, TOO!

GUYS, WE'VE ALWAYS GOT TO BE HONEST
WITH EACH OTHER, AND IF THERE'S A
PROBLEM, WE'VE GOT TO
RESOLVE IT RIGHT AWAY!
DO WE ALL
PROMISE?!

OKAY! I GET THE
MESSAGE!

PROMISE!

THAT DOESN'T MEAN THE GRUMPERS SHOULD GET AWAY WITH IT.

WE'LL DEAL WITH THEM WHEN THE TIME IS RIGHT.

FOR NOW YOU'D BETTER JUST CONCENTRATE ON YOUR FRENCH TEST.

DO YOU WANT A PART IN MY PLAY OR DON'T YOU? THERE'S STILL A LEADING ROLE OPEN! WAIT JUST A COUPLE MORE DAYS, AND YOU'LL BE A STAR!

THERE'S STILL THAT ONE PROBLEM TO SOLVE . . .

. . . THE FRENCH EXAM!

. . . THE FRENCH EXAM!

IF YOU'VE STUDIED, THIS SHOULDN'T BE TOO DIFFICULT! YOU HAVE ONE HOUR . . .

. . . STARTING RIGHT NOW!

IF ONLY IT WAS AN ORAL QUIZ! THEN I COULD USE MY POWERS TO DECIDE WHAT QUESTIONS WOULD BE ASKED!

THEY CAN'T DO THIS TO ME! I HAVE A **RIGHT** TO BE IN THE PLAY, TOO!

DON'T BE MAD AT ME, IRMA!

YOU ALL SAY THAT! SO TELL ME, WHOM SHOULD I BE MAD AT, THEN?

I'M SORRY, BUT THOSE ARE THE RULES! UNTIL YOU'VE GOTTEN YOUR GRADE POINT AVERAGE UP, NO SCHOOL PLAY!

BUT MS. KELLY, UP UNTIL YESTERDAY I WAS ON THE LIST!

LET'S SAY IT WAS AN OVERSIGHT!

AND I WOULD'VE BEEN HAPPY TO CONTINUE OVERLOOKING IT IF THE GRUMPER SISTERS HADN'T POINTED IT OUT TO THE PRINCIPAL!

THOSE TWO AGAIN!

I SWEAR, THIS TIME I'M GOING TO TURN THEM INTO . . . INTO . . . INTO . . .

IS THERE ANYBODY WORSE THAN THE GRUMPER SISTERS?

I REALLY DON'T THINK SO.

DID THE TEST GO BADLY?

I STILL DON'T KNOW! BUT EVERYTHING ELSE IS GOING **TERRIBLY**! NO TRYOUTS FOR ME UNTIL I FIND OUT MY GRADE!

CHEER UP, IRMA! WE'VE GOTTEN THROUGH TOUGHER SITUATIONS. DON'T THINK ABOUT IT NOW, AND GIVE US A NICE SMILE!

I SAID A *SMILE*! YOU DON'T NEED TO START LAUGHING AT ME!

HA-HA-HA! I'M NOT LAUGHING BECAUSE OF YOU . . . HA-HA! HA! SOMETHING IN YOUR JACKET IS SHAKING!

HUH?

HEY! IT'S MY CELL PHONE—IT'S ON VIBRATE!

IT'S BUZZING! IT SOUNDS LIKE MY DAD'S ELECTRIC RAZOR!

BZZZ...

BZZZ...

HELLO? MRS. RUDOLPH? NO, I CAN HEAR YOU. THE CONNECTION'S JUST A LITTLE FUZZY . . .

THEY'VE HAD A DIFFICULT TRIP. I WAS TOLD THEY WOULD BE ARRIVING, BUT SOMETHING HAS GONE WRONG.

THEY DIDN'T COME BY TRAIN, I HOPE! THOSE THINGS ARE NEVER ON TIME!

OF COURSE THEY DIDN'T COME BY TRAIN! THEY CROSSED THROUGH THE VEIL BY WAY OF A PORTAL.

WAIT A SEC! THAT'S A PORTAL?

WHY DIDN'T THE MAP WARN ME?

THAT'S WHAT IT'S DOING RIGHT NOW! LOOK!

OH! FANTASTIC!

HA-HA! BETTER LATE THAN NEVER!

AS I SAID, THERE WAS A PROBLEM DURING THEIR TRIP. ALENA AND MORVAN'S OTHER SON, RESEPH, DISAPPEARED!

HE GOT SCARED WHEN A FREIGHT TRAIN PASSED BY, AND HE RAN OFF!

32

SOUNDS GOOD, WILL . . . BUT SHOULD WE BELIEVE YOU?

LOOK! THESE MUST BE HIS FOOTPRINTS!

AND THEY END HERE! HE MUST'VE CROSSED OVER THE TRACKS.

AND HEATHERFIELD'S DOWN THERE. WE HAVE TO COME UP WITH A PLAN TO FIND HIM.

35

"YEAH, BUT WHERE DO WE START?"

WE'LL HAVE TO SPLIT UP. IF ONLY WE HAD A CLUE WHERE TO LOOK!

HE COULD BE ANYWHERE. AND WITH EVERY MINUTE THAT PASSES, THE SITUATION JUST GETS WORSE AND WORSE.

WE HAVE TO HELP THAT LITTLE BOY! BUT HOW?

THE ONLY PLACE YOU CAN GET THE ANSWERS IS CANDRACAR!

THEN MAYBE WE'D BETTER FIND A WAY TO GET THERE!

MY GRANDMOTHER TOLD ME ABOUT IT ONCE. TO GET THERE, YOU HAVE TO CROSS OVER AN AIR-COLORED BRIDGE!

OKAY! LET'S GET GOING!

ARE YOU KIDDING?

YOU DON'T KNOW WHAT YOU'RE TALKING ABOUT!

YOU'RE RIGHT! I DON'T KNOW! I DON'T KNOW ANYTHING! AND I CAN'T TAKE IT ANY LONGER!

WE HAVE A MAP THAT ONLY WORKS WHEN WE DON'T NEED IT, POWERS WE BARELY UNDERSTAND, AND AN IMPOSSIBLE MISSION!

... AND NOW A LITTLE BOY FROM MERIDIAN HAS DISAPPEARED TO WHO KNOWS WHERE! I DON'T WANT TO TAKE IT ANYMORE!

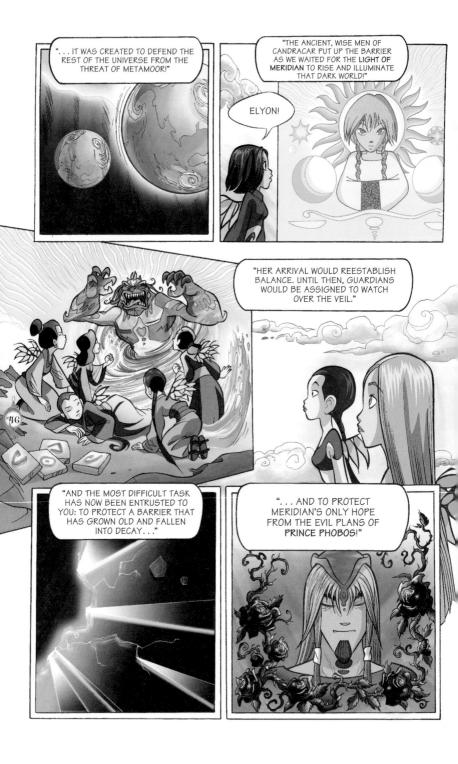

CAN I HELP YOU, GIRLS?

I SURE HOPE SO. WE'RE LOOKING FOR OUR DOG. HIS NAME IS REGINALD.

HE'S LITTLE, WITH WHITE AND BROWN SPOTS.

HMMM . . . NO REGINALD WITH WHITE AND BROWN SPOTS HERE.

HOW ABOUT WITH BROWN AND WHITE SPOTS?

HUH? ARE YOU PLAYING A JOKE ON ME?

WHAT AN ACTRESS!

WHY DO YOU SAY THAT? I'M JUST TRYING TO FIND MY PUPPY!

THIS SHOULD GIVE US A LITTLE TIME.

FLAP FLAP FLAP

ZAP

OH, MY! YOUR PAPERWORK IS FLYING AWAY.

QUIET! SOMEBODY'S DOWN THERE.

RESEPH! ARE YOU HERE? RESEPH!

HI, THERE, YOU CUTE LITTLE PUPPY, YOU!

EPILOGUE:
SHEFFIELD INSTITUTE,
THE NEXT DAY...

YOUR TEST RESULTS WERE DISAPPOINTING, TO SAY THE LEAST.

THERE WAS ONE EXCEPTION. ONE GRADE WAS SURPRISINGLY POSITIVE: IRMA LAIR'S.

HUH?

READ ALOUD TO YOUR CLASSMATES WHAT YOU WROTE, IRMA. CLASS, LISTEN TO WHAT FRENCH **REALLY** SOUNDS LIKE.

YES!

CORNELIA! WILL! I'M A GENIUS!

JE SUIS GENIALE, MERVEILLEUSE, EXTRAORDINAIRE!

SHE PASSED HER TEST!

WAY TO GO, IRMA!

IF THAT'S THE CASE, THEN THERE'S A TRYOUT WAITING FOR YOU!

ALL RIGHT! I LOVE THIS SCHOOL!

GRRRR!

GRR!

HEY THERE! FEROCIOUS LITTLE FELLOW, AREN'T YOU?

GROWWL

WHERE ARE YOU GOING?

YAP YAP YAP

57

SO WHERE DID YOU COME FROM? WHERE'S YOUR OWNER?

YAP YAP YAP

COME HERE, TRIXIE!

THE SHOW'S ABOUT TO START! GET BACK TO YOUR SEAT...

RESEPH!

IT'S STARTING!

"WHAT WILL YOU TELL YOUR GRANDCHILDREN IN YEARS TO COME?"

"OF MAGICAL ADVENTURES IN UNKNOWN LANDS?"

"OF AFFECTION THAT BRINGS TOGETHER DIFFERENT PEOPLE?"

"OF FRIENDSHIP THAT UNITES YOU FOREVER?"

"OR MAYBE . . . OF THE WORST SNOWSTORM IN THE LAST 150 YEARS?"

HAPPY HOLIDAYS!

59

BBBRROOOM

ELYON'S HOUSE, ON THE OUTSKIRTS OF HEATHERFIELD . . .

FROOOSH

THE ELECTRICITY'S OUT. MAYBE WE'D BETTER POSTPONE THE INSPECTION.

I DON'T THINK SO. IT'S NOT EVERY DAY AN ENTIRE FAMILY DISAPPEARS INTO THIN AIR!

WHAT DO WE HAVE HERE?

CRAAACK

ELYON

DRAWINGS BY ELYON BROWN, FROM WHEN SHE WAS SIX UNTIL RIGHT BEFORE HER DISAPPEARANCE. INTERESTING!

HMMM. THERE'S A RECURRING IMAGE. IT LOOKS LIKE A MAGICAL CITY.

LOOK! THIS ONE IS COMPLETE. THE CITY, AGAIN. AND ABOVE IT. . .

. . . A GIRL WEARING A CROWN. FLYING AROUND AND SHINING LIKE THE SUN.

LOOKS LIKE DROPS OF WATER FELL RIGHT ON HER FACE. THE COLORS ARE ALL SMEARED. TOO BAD.

OH, ELYON! WHERE ARE YOU? WHAT HAPPENED TO YOU?

MAY I COME IN?

KNOCK KNOCK

SPEAKING OF SURPRISES, LOOKS LIKE GRANDPA'S LEFT THE HOUSE.

FRUSSHH

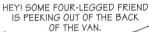

HEY! SOME FOUR-LEGGED FRIEND IS PEEKING OUT OF THE BACK OF THE VAN.

I BET IT'S SOME ABANDONED ANIMAL. FIRST HE NURSES THEM BACK TO HEALTH AND THEN HE DOESN'T KNOW WHERE TO PUT THEM.

HI, KIDS! MAKE WAY FOR AN OLD FRIEND.

WHOOSH

HEY! IT'S HEFTY! THAT'S JACKIE'S PUPPY.

I DON'T USUALLY DOG-SIT, BUT YOUR FRIEND IS GOING TO HELP ME PAY THE BILLS.

WE WERE JUST TALKING ABOUT HER A MINUTE AGO, WEREN'T WE, WILL?

GRRR!

CHEEEP

CHEEEP

WOOF WOOF

MEOOWW

WHAT'S GOTTEN INTO THEM?

HUH?

FAKE! SQUAAAWK! FAAAAKE!

BOW WOW

LATER ON, AT THE SILVER DRAGON, ON THE OTHER SIDE OF TOWN . . .

PLEASE, SIR! LET YOUR DAUGHTER GO OUT. IRMA'S WAITING FOR US.

I'M SORRY, CORNELIA, BUT HAY LIN HAS TO HELP ME CLEAN UP THE RESTAURANT.

WHAT A MESS. I BET IT'S ALL LEFT OVER FROM THE NEW YEAR'S EVE PARTY!

DISTRACT MY DAD! I'LL TAKE CARE OF THE REST.

HAY LIN SAYS YOU'RE SOME KIND OF ORNITHOLOGIST. IS THAT TRUE?

HUH? WELL, I'M NOT EXACTLY AN EXPERT IN BIRDS, BUT I KNOW A THING OR TWO.

I CAN'T SEE VERY WELL THROUGH ALL THIS RAIN. THE BIRD OUT THERE—IS THAT A CROW?

JUST TO SAY IT WITH A BIT OF FLAIR . . . OBEY ME NOW, POWERS OF AIR!

STEP ASIDE, TARANEE.

HAY LIN AND I WILL GET IN BACK. HOP IN FRONT, CORNELIA.

NO!

I MEAN . . . I CAN'T! I HAVE TO . . . UM . . . RUN AN ERRAND. FOR MY MOTHER.

NO PROBLEM, I'LL TAKE YOU. WHERE DO YOU NEED TO GO?

SURE?

I NEED TO WALK THERE, ACTUALLY! TO A RELATIVE'S HOUSE, WHICH IS RIGHT NEAR HERE. I'LL SEE YOU AT IRMA'S, OKAY?

SEE YOU AROUND SOMETIME?

SURE THING! SEE YOU SOON. AND SAY HI TO YOUR FOLKS FOR ME.

I DIDN'T KNOW CORNELIA HAD RELATIVES IN THE NEIGHBORHOOD. DID YOU?

ALL I KNOW . . .

. . . IS THAT WHEN SHE'S AROUND YOUR BROTHER, SHE SUDDENLY GETS VERY PECULIAR.

THAT HURTS, ELYON. I'M THE ONLY PERSON YOU CAN TRUST COMPLETELY.

OH, REALLY? FINE! THEN TELL ME WHERE MY HOME IS. BECAUSE IT'S NOT THE ONE OUT THERE!

I USED TO HAVE A MOTHER AND FATHER. I HAD FRIENDS AND . . .

BUT THEN YOU DIDN'T HAVE A KINGDOM TO TAKE CARE OF. YOU'RE JUST AFRAID.

BUT DON'T WORRY; I'M HERE FOR YOU. AND NOTHING IS STRONGER THAN THE BOND OF A BROTHER.

PRINCE PHOBOS!

WOULD YOU LIKE CEDRIC TO LEAVE **FOREVER**, MY DEAR SISTER?

78

THANK YOUR LUCKY STARS, YOU FOOL. WAIT FOR ME IN THE GARDEN.

YES, MY LORD!

N—NO! I'M JUST SO CONFUSED. I'LL SPEAK WITH HIM LATER.

PHOBOS? I'M THE LIGHT OF MERIDIAN, RIGHT?

THAT IS THE TITLE THAT AWAITS YOU—THE TITLE THAT WILL SOON BE YOURS!

PHOBOS'S SINISTER PLOT IS REFLECTED IN THE GRIM SKIES OVER MERIDIAN...

... AND EVEN THE SKY IN HEATHERFIELD IS FAR FROM CHEERY...

BRROOOOOUUUM

MOM!

MOM! THE POT IS WHISTLING!

SO, SING, IRMA. THAT WAY WE'LL HAVE A NICE LITTLE CHORUS GOING!

A CHORUS! HEE-HEE-HEE! A NICE LITTLE CHORUS!

NOW I KNOW WHY WE HAVE CHRISTOPHER. YOU NEEDED SOMEONE WHO WOULD LAUGH AT YOUR JOKES!

OF COURSE! YOU AND YOUR FATHER ARE SUCH A TERRIBLE AUDIENCE.

HAND ME THE SALT, PLEASE.

YOU MADE ZUCCHINI? BUT I TOLD YOU CORNELIA DOESN'T LIKE ZUCCHINI.

SO? YOU DON'T LIKE CORNELIA!

WHAT DO YOU KNOW, SQUIRT? SO WE'VE HAD A FEW ARGUMENTS! SO WHAT?

DON'T SAY MEAN THINGS, CHRISTOPHER. ESPECIALLY WHEN WE HAVE COMPANY OVER.

SPEAKING OF COMPANY... CHRISTOPHER, TAKE THESE APPETIZERS INTO THE DINING ROOM. OUR GUESTS MUST BE HUNGRY.

GOOD! LITTLE MR. BUTTINSKY IS OUT OF MY HAIR.

THE GIRLS SHOULD BE HERE ANY MINUTE. I HAVE TO WARN THEM ABOUT THE NASTY SURPRISE WAITING FOR THEM . . .

"EVEN IF THEY'RE NOT ALL HERE YET."

HEY! WAIT UP!

WILL!

LOOK WHO'S HERE! WHY THE SAD PUPPY DOG FACE?

DON'T TALK TO ME ABOUT ANIMALS, OKAY?

OOOH! SOMETHING TELLS ME WE'D BETTER AVOID ANY TOPIC RELATED TO ANIMALS AND MATT!

HA-HA! ERY FUNNY. ≀, EVERYTHING AS A TOTAL ASTER AT THE T SHOP. BUT WORST THING WAS WHAT PENED BACK AT MY HOUSE . . .

"MOM SAID WE HAD TO TALK ABOUT SOMETHING IMPORTANT, WITH MR. COLLINS!"

I'M SO GLAD I HAD THE EXCUSE THAT IRMA INVITED ME TO DINNER.

WHY? DIDN'T YOU SAY MR. COLLINS WAS GETTING TO BE ALMOST NICE?

THERE'S A HUGE DIFFERENCE BETWEEN A NICE GUY AND A FATHER!

OH, COME ON! DO YOU THINK THEY WANTED TO TELL YOU THEY'RE ENGAGED? ISN'T THAT A LITTLE SOON?

SORRY TO INTERRUPT, BUT WE HAVE A LITTLE PROBLEM IN HERE!

HUH?

WHAT?

WILL! THOSE AGENTS WE MET AT IRMA'S ARE **STAKED OUT** AT MY HOUSE.

WHAT? DO THEY THINK YOU HAD SOMETHING TO DO WITH ELYON'S DISAPPEARANCE?

I DON'T KNOW. I MUST HAVE MADE THEM SUSPICIOUS LAST NIGHT. THE MINUTE I GO OUTSIDE, THEY'LL START FOLLOWING ME.

SO WHAT? YOU'VE GOT NOTHING TO HIDE, RIGHT?

BUT TODAY WE HAVE TO GO TO ELYON'S HOUSE AND CLOSE THE PORTAL IN THE BASEMENT.

RIGHT! I TOTALLY FORGOT ABOUT THAT.

I'LL COME OVER AND HELP YOU SOON. BUT FIRST I HAVE TO STOP BY THE PET SHOP FOR A SECOND . . .

". . . AND DO ONE LITTLE THING . . ."

THERE WE GO. MY ROOM'S SPOTLESS. MOM CAN'T HAVE ANYTHING ELSE TO SAY . . .

WILL! THERE'S SOMETHING I HAVE TO TELL YOU.

JEEZ! MY MISTAKE.

KNOCK KNOCK

ACTUALLY, I SHOULD'VE TOLD YOU LAST NIGHT. BUT YOU WERE AT IRMA'S AND...

AND YOU WERE AT MR. COLLINS'S. SO I'D SAY WE'RE EVEN!

DEAN WAS HELPING ME WITH AN IMPORTANT DECISION.

YEAH, RIGHT. I BET.

PLEASE, WILL...

HER VOICE! IT SOUNDS LIKE SHE'S CRYING! MAYBE I'D BETTER NOT PUSH IT.

I'LL OPEN UP! BUT I'M TELLING YOU RIGHT NOW, I DON'T WANT TO SEE ANY TEARS, AND...

T-CLUNK

...VATHEK?

BATH... WHAT?

"SHE CAME TO SEE US AT NIGHT, PUTTING HER OWN LIFE AT RISK AND BRAVING THE UNDERGROUND WORLD OF THE ENDLESS CITY."

IF YOU'RE LOOKING FOR CALEB, HE'S OUT RECRUITING REBELS IN YOUR NAME.

I'M HERE FOR HELP, VATHEK. YOU HAVE TO HELP ME FREE MY ADOPTIVE PARENTS.

I KNOW THAT I DISOWNED THEM, BUT I'VE ALSO SEEN WHERE THEY'RE BEING KEPT. IT'S A HORRIBLE PLACE!

THE PRISON IS A CREATION OF YOUR BROTHER'S. THEY LOCK UP ANYONE WHO THINKS DIFFERENTLY FROM HIM!

THEY'RE SUFFERING. I CAN FEEL IT. THEY'LL NEVER SURVIVE UNTIL MY CORONATION.

NO ONE CAN BREAK INTO THE PRISON, NOT EVEN ME! YOU SHOULD ASK THE GUARDIANS FOR HELP.

NO! EXCEPT FOR CORNELIA, THEY ALL HATE ME! THEY WON'T HELP ME!

99

HMMM . . . I'M NOT EXACTLY A GENIUS . . .

. . . BUT IT'S EASY TO SEE THAT IF YOU'VE COME ALL THE WAY HERE, ELUDING PHOBOS'S CONTROL, IT MEANS THAT YOU MIGHT BE DOUBTING HIM.

PERHAPS THE MOMENT HAS COME TO BELIEVE IN SOMEONE ELSE, LIGHT OF MERIDIAN!

S—SORRY. I DIDN'T THINK I'D SEE YOU HERE. DIDN'T YOU HAVE BAND OR SOMETHING?

THE DRUMMER ISN'T FEELING WELL, SO I THOUGHT I'D FEED THE ANIMALS.

BUT . . . I WAS SUPPOSED TO DO THAT.

WELL, YEAH. I MEAN, I KNEW THAT. THAT'S WHY I STOPPED BY, ACTUALLY.

I WAS JUST WONDERING . . . ARE YOU FREE TONIGHT?

HUH? ARE YOU KIDDING? OF COURSE I'M . . .

. . . NO! THAT IS . . . MAYBE. UM . . . IT DEPENDS!

WHAT CAN I SAY? I HAVE TO GO TO ANOTHER WORLD FIRST?

THAT'S MY GRANDFATHER! HE SAID HE WOULDN'T BE BY UNTIL LATER.

UM . . . WE . . . WE JUST CAME HERE TOGETHER!

NO! YEAH! MAYBE! IT DEPENDS! YOU'RE ALWAYS SO MYSTERIOUS AND . . . HUH?

ACTUALLY, WE HAVE AN ERRAND TO RUN. YEAH. WE HAVE TO . . . UM . . . TO GET . . . UM . . .

A MILLION EXCUSES LATER, IN FRONT OF CORNELIA'S APARTMENT...

I'M STARTING TO THINK THAT YOU MIGHT HAVE MADE A MISTAKE, MEDINA.

CORNELIA'S HIDING SOMETHING, MCTIENNAN. I'M SURE OF IT!

THE ONLY THING I'M SURE ABOUT IS THAT WE DON'T HAVE ANY LEADS.

THIS STAKEOUT IS USELESS AND...

HI, THERE!

DO YOU THINK YOU COULD TELL ME WHAT THAT PEDAL IS USED FOR? THE ONE ON THE LEFT?

THAT'S THE CLUTCH, SIR.

AHA! I THOUGHT SO. AND I BET YOU PUSH THAT ONE BEFORE CHANGING GEARS!

WHAT IS GOING ON?

DON'T ASK! JUST GET IN THE CAR.

THIS WAY, MCTIENNAN! I KNOW I SAW A LIGHT COMING FROM THE BASEMENT.

THAT'S STRANGE. THE ELECTRICITY'S OUT.

HI! WHAT BRINGS YOU FOLKS HERE?

WE THOUGHT YOU MIGHT BE HERE.

BUT WE COULD ASK YOU THE SAME QUESTION.

LATER ON, IN FRONT OF CORNELIA'S HOUSE . . .

THANKS FOR GOING WITH ME, WILL. THANKS FOR EVERYTHING!

NO PROBLEM! THE IMPORTANT THING IS THAT WE SHOOK OFF THOSE AGENTS.

DO YOU THINK THEY BOUGHT THE STORY ABOUT HAVING A GET-TOGETHER IN MEMORY OF ELYON AT HER HOUSE?

I DOUBT IT. BUT I COULDN' COME WITH ANYTH BETTER

". . . AND AGENT MEDINA REALLY SHOWED US HOW TOUGH SHE WAS."

LET'S JUST GO! WE HAVE NO REASON TO KEEP THE GIRLS ANY LONGER.

I'M TELLING YOU, THERE WAS A GIANT IN THE BACK OF THIS VAN. A REAL MONSTER AND . . .

YEAH, YOU'RE RIGHT! THAT'S ONE GIANT. . . DOG!

WOOF WOOF